AMOS AHOY!

A COUCH ADVENTURE ON LAND AND SEA

by **SUSAN SELIGSON**
and **HOWIE SCHNEIDER**

Little, Brown and Company
Boston Toronto London

For Don Brown

First Edition

Library of Congress Cataloging-in-Publication Data

Seligson, Susan.
   Amos ahoy! : a couch adventure on land and sea / by Susan Seligson
and Howie Schneider. — 1st ed.
   p. cm.
   Summary: When Amos the dog accidentally disturbs the neighborhood bully, he sets off a
high-speed chase through town with everyone from the dog catcher to a used-furniture salesman
hot on his trail.
   ISBN 0-316-77403-0
   [1. Dogs—Fiction. 2. Furniture—Fiction. 3. Bullies—Fiction.]
   I. Schneider, Howie, 1930- . II. Title.
   PZ7.S456946Alzb   1990
   [E]—dc20   90-4011
                                                                                      CIP
                                                                                       AC

Joy Street Books are published
by Little, Brown and Company (Inc.)

10 9 8 7 6 5 4 3 2 1
HR

Published simultaneously in Canada
by Little, Brown & Company (Canada) Limited

Printed in the United States of America

Amos is an old dog.
He is so old that he spends almost all his time
on the couch.

But his life has been far
from dull since the day he
discovered that with a flick
of his paw he could make
his couch MOVE!

VAROOM...

SWAT!

CRASH!

Ever since then

Amos always has fun

wherever he goes.

When Amos returns from his daily outings,

Mr. and Mrs. Bobson always have his supper waiting.

Then it's time for a nice nap before bed.

Early one morning, Amos woke up looking forward to his usual routine—a visit to the playground, a swing through the park, and a snack at his friend Benny's hot-dog stand.

As he revved up his couch, Mrs. Bobson said, "Come home early, Amos.

VAROOM

We're going on a special trip tomorrow, and I want you to be well rested."

It was a cloudy and breezy day.
Amos glided down the street,
his ears flapping in the wind.
"I'll just go for a short spin," he decided.

Up ahead, Chops,
the neighborhood
bully, was enjoying
a snack . . .

which Amos accidentally
interrupted . . .

BLAM!

in a very unfortunate way.

SPLAT!

Amos began to quiver.
"Uh-oh. I think Chops is a little annoyed."

But he didn't stay to find out.

For the first time ever,
Amos drove right past Benny's hot-dog stand.
Chops was right
behind him.

Benny's customer never even had a chance to taste his hot dog.

Chops had picked the wrong person to knock over.

"I'll catch you, you miserable hound, "
cried the dog catcher. And he jumped into his truck.

Meanwhile, Amos was beginning to get tired.
"I have to find a place to hide," he thought.

"Oh boy, this house looks like a good place!"
And in he scooted.

"Wow! They sure have a lot of pets in this family."

Suddenly Amos knew why all these animals were here.

"This is not a family. These pets are patients!" he realized, and shot out the door. But Chops was still looking for him, and he was madder than ever.

Down the street, Sam the furniture man and his helper were loading their truck when Amos came speeding by.

"Look!" cried Sam, spotting Amos. "I could get a lot of money for a couch like THAT." He jumped into his truck and joined the chase, heading toward the river.

Amos started across the bridge. "Can't stop for a snack," he thought, mistaking the toll booth for a hot-dog stand.

Amos had never driven over such a big bridge. "Why is the road suddenly hanging in the air?" he wondered.

Officer Barnes could not believe her eyes. "Hey, you guys haven't paid the toll!" she yelled. "Time for me to go to work." She hopped onto her motorcycle.

When he got to the other side, Amos began to worry. He was getting far from home. To make matters worse, it was starting to rain.

Amos didn't know which way to turn. So he took a chance and followed a line of cars . . .

right onto a ferryboat.

Amos had never been on a ferry before. "What's going on?" he wondered. "How come I'm not moving but I'm moving?"

The ferry pulled away from shore. The dog catcher grabbed Chops, and Officer Barnes gave a ticket to Sam the furniture man. Finally, Amos was safe.

It began to rain harder and harder.
The boat tossed in the waves.

"I'd better move inside," thought Amos.
"My couch will get soaked."

He was just beginning to relax when a lady plunked herself down next to him, opened her bag, and started to feed her little dog.

"Gee, I'm pretty hungry too," thought Amos. So he rocked his couch, sending a few tasty snacks his way.

HERE YOU GO, SWEETIE

"My, my, the seas are very rough today," said the lady. "I believe I'm a little seasick." And she took her little dog and left.

The ferry lurched to one side, and before Amos knew it . . .

he had another visitor.

But the friendship was brief.

Then Amos heard something familiar.

AMOS! AMOS! AMOS! WHERE ARE YOU?

"Someone on the ferry is calling me!" he thought.

"Here I am," barked Amos, racing out onto the deck. But nobody paid any attention.

The ferry rocked and pitched in the storm.

Amos slid from side to side.
Suddenly he heard a cry.

HELP!

OH, MY
GOSH...

CRASH

Amos quickly revved up his couch, threw it in gear, and backed up just in time.

Once again he had company.

"You saved him!
You saved my Amos!"
a woman cried, rushing
to hug the little boy at
Amos's side.

"This dog is a hero,"
the captain declared.
"But whose dog
are you?"

No one seemed to know. The captain inspected
Amos's tag. "Hey, you're an Amos, too," he said.
Amos smiled proudly.

Soon people were feeding him hot dogs and lining up
to pat his head. "This is fun," thought Amos.

It was only when the ferry finally reached shore that Amos thought of the Bobsons. "It's almost dark. If I don't get home soon, they'll worry."

The whole crew came out to wave good-bye.

When Amos got home, the Bobsons were relieved to see him.
He had never been out in such a bad storm before.

They gave him some chicken soup and put him to bed.
"We're taking you someplace new tomorrow,"
Mrs. Bobson reminded him.

"It's going to be a big surprise."

It certainly was.

And not just for Amos.